GW00468015

The Dire Dark

Shacklebound Books Anthologies

Eric Fomley

Published by Shacklebound Books, 2022.

THE DIRE DARK

First edition. November 8, 2022.

ISBN: 979-8215867082

Written by Eric Fomley.

Table of Contents

Also by Shacklebound Books 1

Dreaming War | Marisca Pichette 3

Dousing the Fire | Alyson Tait.. 11

Last Trick | Gordon Linzner 13

Roses and Vipers | Lisa Short.. 19

Weathering, the Storms of Time | Jenna Hanchey.............. 25

To the Water Goes My Pain | Addison Smith 31

New Year's Skeleton | Larry Hodges..................................... 37

The Nature of the Beast | Ed Ahern...................................... 41

Harriers | A. P. Howell 47

A Life to Spare | Fulvio Gatti 51

Greenwich, Noon | Liam Hogan 57

Shackled for Eternity | Kai Delmas 63

Chrysopoeia | Dawn Vogel... 65

With Fire and Axes | DJ Tyrer.. 67

Conscripted | Thomas J. Griffin 73

For Cassy, my better half.

Also by Shacklebound Books

Shacklebound Books Drabble Anthologies
Drabbledark: An Anthology of Dark Drabbles
Drabbledark II: An Anthology of Dark Drabbles
Chronos: An Anthology of Time Drabbles
Wyrms: An Anthology of Dragon Drabbles
Short Horror Stories

Shacklebound Books Flash Fiction Anthologies
Timeshift: Tales of Time
Sins and Other Worlds
Maelstroms
Dread Space
The Mods

Other Drabble Publications
Martian: Year One
Dystopia Drabble Showcase

1

SFF Excursions
War Torn
War Pawns

Dreaming War
Marisca Pichette

We were wolves, once.

I walk across the fields that abut the mountains' feet, feeling the hardness of the ground where my ancestors once hunted with claws and teeth. A winter separates that age from ours, the time of fur and packs as distant as the Shornbacks' territory far to the south. My harvest from the day is strapped to my back, a basket of potatoes coated in coal-black soil, smelling still strongly of the earth.

Tonight the moon is like a cat's pupil, its slivered black gaze watching from above, iris pocked and white. As I near our village I drop onto all fours, quickening my pace, heading for the light of the fires.

Our village grows from the mountains at its back, rocks tumbling down into caves and pillars carved with stories that glow when the moon finds them. In the light of the night wolves dance, wolves hunt.

We do not dance anymore. We do not hunt. Looking at the pillars reaching up into the night, I wonder—not for the first time—what it was like to live before the winter that spanned a millennium. A winter that changed us from what we once were into something more, and less.

I trot past our village's gate and into the fire's warmth. In the soft blue light emanating from the pillars I see Grandmother sitting with my brothers near the center of the village. I drop my basket onto the hard-packed soil and it leans, coming to a rest against the base of one of the pillars. Black soil colors the grey-blue ground like storm clouds over a twilight sky.

Grandmother looks up as I approach. She is balding, the hair that was once thick retreating from her limbs in shreds of grey and white. I enter the ring of light that holds her along with my two brothers, Mais and Horj. Grandmother pauses in the story she was telling before I arrived and waits until I am crouching beside them. Smoke in my nose smothering all other scents, Grandmother tells us of our ancestors.

"We grew from pups. Our teeth were longer, sharper, honed each time we tracked a prey to its end." Grandmother spreads her arms, skin hanging diaphanous from her thin frame. Her eyes glitter yellow in the firelight. "Our ancestors knew every track in the dust," she says, "every pebble on the lake's shore."

Grandmother pauses, and I think about how we have changed. I can smell better than a Shornback, and run faster, too. But the purity of what we once were has been lost to time.

There is no longer a lake between our civilization and the Shornbacks' territory in the south. Where our ancestors prowled around black waters there is now a trench of barren soil. Not even potatoes can grow there. And on the other side—Shornbacks.

My gaze wanders to the pillars shining around us. Along with the once-hunt they depict the war that came before the winter. Wolves not chasing, but being chased across stone, pursued by Shornbacks bearing axes, wearing wolfskins.

The outcome of the war was never decided. Instead the world shook, cracked open and filled the sky with smoke as black as soil. And the winter came. We fled to the mountains and learned to live on fungus instead of meat. Over the centuries, our bodies changed.

"Siku," Grandmother says, her voice the sound of wind in grass. I pull my gaze from the pillar and look into her wrinkled face. "You are thinking about the winter's end," she murmurs.

I nod and look down at my feet, not so different from a Shornback's. When the winter ended and our people emerged, they thought the Shornbacks would not have survived the long winter. But they did.

Grandmother nods. She tilts her snout to the moon. "And so the war continues."

Grandmother stands, her body moving smoothly despite her age. She lopes away, leaving us circled around the dying fire, exchanging looks that say nothing. I turn my eyes to the moon.

Ama is the name Mother gave to the moon. It has always captured me, the slit than grows and grows but never fills. Ama swings between brightness, a black disc the center of its pendulum path. On one end, it fills until it is a hair away from total revelation. On the other, it is a sliver of light pushed to the edge of a shadow world.

I have never seen it fill all the way. We sleep when the moon completes itself, when the spirits rise. When the wolves come back to hunt.

Tonight is the apex, the night before Ama completes its cycle. I rub my arms, flattening the hairs that stand on-end in the cold.

A restlessness chews at me as I stand and follow my brothers to our cave. For the first time, I feel a strong urge to run—away from the village, away from the mountains. I want to run all the way across the miles of open land that separate our civilization from the Shornbacks'. And at the end of that journey—what will I find?

I pause at the cave mouth and turn back to the night. Tomorrow, the ancestors continue the war that no winter, no death can stop.

"Siku," Mais calls from inside our cave. "Come inside. The blessing will not come if you are out here all night."

The blessing. My stomach flutters. It has been a month since we last tasted meat. Tomorrow's feast brings me back from the edge, and I turn away from the fires and retreat into darkness, to sleep.

BUT I DO NOT SLEEP for long. After what feels like only a minute, my eyes open. While my brothers are resting, I roll onto all fours, and run.

Down the mountain's foot, skirting the edge of the village cloaked in the smoke of dying fires, the pillars gleaming blue beacons in the dark. I run past them, my shadow leading me south. I run faster than I've ever run, ignoring the scrapes of rocks on my hands, the scrabbling of my toes each time I slip.

As the village fades behind me, I hear them.

Howls fill the night and suddenly I am singing with the ancestors, singing a song of war. I run, the mountains shrinking behind me, the night cast in the glow of the near-full body of the moon.

But no. When I look up, Ama is a perfect sphere, a face bone-white and deadly. A mask of war.

When I look ahead, my shadow is no longer visible. Wolves made of moonlight run ahead of me, a pack of beauty and determination lighting my way.

I do not know how long or how far we ran together before the horizon flares with fire. The ancestors howl and I howl with them, my own voice unfamiliar in this altered world. The fire on the horizon brightens as we enter a territory as different from us as Ama is from the sun.

A crack splits across the night. The Shornbacks have seen us coming.

MORNING. I TWITCH, the echo of a scream cut off as sleep leaves me. Someone is moving nearby, speaking with my brother's voice. I stir and open my eyes to find myself on my mat in my cave. Was it a dream?

"Siku, get up," Mais calls. "It is starting."

I roll onto my side, the images from last night flying away from me. I gasp as I try to stand, my legs quivering. I struggle upright, flexing my shoulders and wincing at the way they pull under my skin. If what I experienced was a dream, it afforded me no rest.

I walk shakily behind my brothers down to the village. A large fire blazes in the blessing pit and Grandmother is singing, her chin raised, her teeth blunt and bared. I look at her, and then my eyes wander to the struts suspended over the fire, their burdens shining in the sun. At the sight of them, I am not exhilarated as I usually am, when this monthly blessing comes. Instead all I hear is dream howling, and my muscles ache.

The Shornbacks hang from skinny ankles, their hairless arms limp and stiff above their heads. The ancestors have gifted us ten of the creatures, their throats emptied of blood, their entrails piled by the fire. Grandmother circles the offering, her claws unsheathed and translucent in the sunrise.

"The war continues," she chants, her voice dipping in and out of a growl, "and our ancestors are victorious. Siku!"

I jump at my name. Grandmother turns to me, her lips still peeled back. She raises her arms and I mimic her, my shoulders aching with the action. When I look up at my hands, my claws are not translucent, but stained red.

"Siku," Grandmother calls, her declaration buoyed by the wind. "You are now Siku Kali. You have joined the ancestors in dream-war, and you have triumphed at their side.

"The wolves live on inside you."

The ancestors run across moonlit grass. Their phantasmal howls echo in my mind.

We remember the wolves, and they remember us.

MARISCA PICHETTE writes about monsters and possibility. Her collection, *Rivers in Your Skin, Sirens in Your Hair,* is forthcoming in Spring 2023.

Dousing the Fire
Alyson Tait

J ust after sunset, Delilah lit a silver candle and prayed, "Today the earth grows colder, and the wind blows faster. Fires dwindle smaller, and rain falls harder. Gods above, please help the light of the sun find its way back home."

She'd spent the day drinking and eating with friends. Now, however, a howling wind slapped against the windows, interrupting her Yuletide celebration. The candle flickered in response, and Delilah fidgeted.

A nagging voice whispered, 'the ritual is wrong.'

To quiet her doubts, she adjusted sprigs of holly and put a pinecone in its box — only to return it to the altar. She set a gold saucer onto a gold-rimmed dinner plate. The long night ahead made her uneasy. Legends battled in her mind like gods and demons.

Had she prayed to the right side?

A crack of thunder startled Delilah, her elbow bumping the altar—causing the candle to wobble in its stand.

"Oh, for Odin's sake," she cursed.

Lightning answered, and her feeble flame flickered before darkness engulfed the room, electricity dying with the fire.

She screamed when the next strike revealed a set of horns and glistening eyes.

A final flash of white-hot light and her athame floated above her altar. Searing pain in both eyes followed the image, plunging her into permanent darkness.

"Your gods are dead, and your sun will never shine again," the creature spoke between waves of thunder. "Happy winter solstice, witch."

Its saliva landed on Delilah's face like rain.

ALYSON TAIT has appeared in *(mac)ro(mic)* and *Wrongdoing Magazine*, among others. You can find her on Twitter @rudexvirus1 or at AlysonTait.com.

Last Trick
Gordon Linzner

Marigen Randol, merchant-prince of Stolkin, paused at the door of his special storeroom to expel an agonized gasp. He felt as though splinters had been driven under the fingernails of his right hand. The muscles in those digits spasmed.

Randol stifled his outcry, to deny Varen the satisfaction of hearing his scream. He'd learned to bear much pain in the past ten years. Soon enough, the torments would end.

From without, this storeroom was indistinguishable from the others in Randol's sub-basement. Inside, however, it was smaller, because the walls were two layers of stone thicker. Every cubic meter in the other rooms was required for the storage of imported silks, exotic carvings, and similar bulky items of trade; this one stood empty most of the time. When in use, it easily held two or three men, a set of chains, a brazier of flaming coals and an assortment of irons for heating.

Randol buried the pain-struck hand in the crimson folds of his cloak, rapping on the door with his left. In response, a small panel slid aside. Two eyes, circled by black, peered out.

"He still lives," Marigen stated. He did not have to ask. He knew.

The panel slid shut and the door creaked inward. The merchant-prince entered stiffly, nodding at his servant. The latter was a brawny man, stripped to the waist save for the black hood over his head.

"Aren't you hot in that thing?" Randol asked. The hood covered all but the eyes, so the merchant could not see the man's obligatory smile. Everyone appreciated the master's humor; they had to.

"I don't want him..." the servant began.

"...to know your face. A wise precaution. He still wields considerable power. Has he spoken yet?"

"Volumes, but nothing on the subject that concerns you. He has endured the irons for three days without food or water. His stubbornness has cost him his right eye and a hole in the cheek. I think he will not talk. You should slay him and end your misery."

Randol looked at the man chained spread-eagled to the dank wall. His slim, pale body was a mass of welts, burns, and scars. His remaining eye glared hatefully at the merchant.

"I agree," said Randol.

"Then I shall..."

"No. I promised this day to myself. Leave us."

The hooded one bowed and backed out of the chamber, closing the door after him. Randol stepped toward his prisoner.

"Enjoying yourself, Varen?"

Varen seemed hardly to hear the words, but needles of pain shot up the merchant's left leg. The knee buckled. Randol moaned and cursed his foolishness in baiting the mage, however tempting the opportunity.

When he'd regained his breath, Randol said, "You have put spells on me and mine."

"Several," Varen admitted in a barely audible voice. "Sometimes simultaneously."

"Yes. My arthritis is your latest work, though not your worst."

Varen smiled again. "Which was the worst? The loss of your richest caravan in a desert storm? Your daughter's running off with the king of thieves...to subsequently be hung alongside him? The mildew that infests every corridor of your palace?"

"Enough!" The merchant glared at Varen. If only he dared strike the magician...! Absurd that a man chained, starved, tortured almost to death should still be able to harm him! Yet Varen had that power; Randol felt it in every twinge.

"No matter," the mage concluded. "Your favorites would no doubt differ from mine."

Randol tasted blood from his own bit lip. "You were clever, Varen. Seven years passed before I even suspected my bad luck was due not to fate but a wizard's malice. Then to find an oracle capable of discovering you... I met a lot of charlatans along the way. Once you were identified, of course, I had you captured...at the cost of three score highly-paid mercenaries."

"Whom you now do not have to pay."

"That's irrelevant."

"Will torturing me for three days make up for a decade of my jests?"

"Of course not. Since you will not be persuaded to cease, my only recourse against your sorcery is to slay you. I know spells cannot survive their creator. You would be dead already, but there is a puzzle only you can answer." Randol stepped closer. "I ask again why you have done this to me."

"I don't like you."

Randol spat. "Obviously. Why not?"

Varen shook his head. "That's part of my revenge. You have many skeletons in your closet; pick one. Perhaps you don't recall the act. What does a... No. You'll never know."

Randol shrugged. "I suppose not. I'll chalk it up to unmotivated spite. It won't matter once I'm free of you."

The merchant reached for the rag-wrapped end of the iron his man had most recently used on Varen. Its other end had cooled from white-hot to red, but that meant nothing. Randol required the shape, long and tapering to a point, more than the temperature.

Before the mage could invoke another crippling attack, Randol rushed forward. The tip ripped Varen's abdomen.

Thick though the walls were, Varen's screech faintly penetrated to the next level of the sub-cellar. Only a few rats were there to hear it.

Randol yanked the iron sideways, tearing tissue and flesh. Then he stepped back, sweating. His fingers began to cramp. He looked at Varen in dismay.

"Still you live!"

Varen's voice came weakly; the merchant strained to hear him.

"Not for long. I must tell you a thing."

"Ah, now you confess!"

"Not at all. I foresaw this day. I knew I'd be caught and slain. It pleases me that you have authored your own destruction." The mage gulped air and continued swiftly, trying to get all said before he could say no more. "Six years ago you contracted a cancer. I would not let you go so easily; I bespelled that malignancy to keep it in abeyance. When I die, so die all my spells. Your cancer will make up for lost time. You will suffer six years of deterioration in minutes!"

"You lie to save your life."

"With my guts hanging out? We are both dead men." Varen coughed blood, spasmed, and hung unmoving from his chains.

Marigen Randol threw the iron to the stone floor. The clatter echoed in the still room. The merchant yanked open the door and rushed to the stairs. Why had the oracle not foreseen this? What one magic-weaver accomplished, so could another. He needed to find a mage to renew Varen's protective spell.

Malignant cells coursed like molten lead through his body. As his boots scraped the top step, before he entered the palace proper, Randol knew further flight was useless. His vocal cords had been eaten away. Before he could make his needs known by gestures or written word, he would be dead. With a silent sob of defeat, Marigen Randol, merchant-prince of Stolkin, sat at the head of the stairs, head bowed, feeling the cancer tighten about his lungs and waiting for death.

When the last breath came, there was just one thing on his mind.

Why?

Last Trick originally appeared in The Argonaut #11 in 1984.

GORDON LINZNER founder *Space and Time Magazine*, author three novels, scores of short stories *F&SF*, etc. Member HWA and SFWA.

Roses and Vipers
Lisa Short

The fountain chuckled softly in the moonless dark. Traces of the crossroads where it had once offered water to thirsty travelers still remained beneath a wild tangle of weeds and bramble. The fountain itself was oddly untouched by the undergrowth rioting in silence all around it; no moss grew on the tiny, ornate carvings of roses and vipers that squirmed along the edges of its basin.

Some distance away, a branch cracked, the sharp report echoing through the trees; a youthful voice cried, *"Ouch!"* and a second voice, scarcely older, scolded, "Hush! You'll scare her away."

"Are we sneaking up on her, then? In that case, we might as well have gone back home an hour ago—"

"Shh!"

The muffled sounds of passage grew nearer, then nearer still, until two girls burst into the clearing. One clutched a lantern; its roughly swinging light reflected off the black rivulets of water bubbling undisturbed down the tall stone spire. Both girls gazed in astonishment around them, then at the fountain. "Drat," said the taller girl, lowering the lantern. "We're lost."

The other aimed an accusing stare up at her companion. "What do you mean, we're lost? How do you know?"

"Have you ever seen this clearing before? I certainly haven't."

"No-ooo..." The smaller girl's stare returned to the fountain, peaceful beneath the lantern's soft golden glow. "Grandmother's stories!"

"'Grandmother's stories?'" her companion remarked dryly. "That's an interesting new way to swear. Better than the other ways you've been experimenting with lately, I suppose—"

"No, no, Grandmother's *stories!* Remember? The one about the clan chieftain's son who married the girl who'd been cursed by a fa—"

"Linette."

"What?"

"If you're thirsty, now is a fine time for you to have a drink, but we are not standing here for hours discussing some old tale Grandmother told you. We have a cow, *and* a way home, to find."

"Oh, a drink," said a third voice, very softly, and both girls froze. "A drink, for a fine lady? Or a poor goodwife?" They looked around wildly, but the clearing was empty save for themselves and the fountain. "It's been so long, so long..." The voice died away, sighing.

"Petra," Linette moaned. Petra yanked her sister close to her side, lantern held out before her like a shield, stilling when a flicker of movement caught her eye. Linette spotted it a second later and gasped, pointing.

In the formless dark beneath the basin, something was unfolding. It straightened up abruptly, and wide dark eyes gleamed at them from the shadow of a ragged hood. "Good girls," said the voice—it was a fair voice, strangely at odds with the flickering darkness of the eyes. "Have you a silver pitcher, to give me a drink?"

"N—" Petra began, then *oof*ed as her sister elbowed her in the stomach.

"We—we don't, good lady," Linette said, voice trembling. "We were only out looking for Dilys, you see—our cow. We have nothing with which to give you water."

Petra suddenly remembered the tale—one of Grandmother's endless fables, yes, about the old kingdoms, before all their country had fallen to one king, a foreigner in a faraway land. It hadn't been a clan chieftain's son, but a king's, and it hadn't been one cursed girl, but two...*sisters*. One so courteous and one so disobliging, and the fairy had—Petra stared whitely at the small sharp carvings at the fountain's edge, that almost seemed to move in the lantern's unsteady light. The rose petals unfolding, the viper tails lashing—

"And you?" The dark eyes slid to Petra's face. "What do you say...pretty girl?" The shadows beneath the hood shifted into a smile like a sickle.

"We regret," Petra whispered, then swallowed and said more strongly, "We regret we have nothing to serve you water in. Good lady. We were not getting water at all." She must match Linette, in courtesy and sincerity—*not* exceed her, *not* fall short—

"But I heard you!" cried the Thing, in tones of false cheer. "I heard you tell your sister to have a drink, from this very fountain!"

21

"I only meant her to drink from her own hand." Beside her, Linette began to cry silently. Not knowing what else to do, Petra said rapidly, "We could each put our hands together, and you might drink out of that. If you wished?"

The Thing's smile widened. "Clever girls. What gifts would suit for such clever mouths? Indeed, good children, I am *very* thirsty."

Slowly, Petra set the lantern down on the ground and groped for her sister's hand, tugging her closer to the fountain. Linette's shaking fingers curled into a cup, and Petra pressed her own fingers up tightly beside them; together, they dipped their hands into the basin and drew up a scant mouthful of the icy water. The Thing glided forward; the ragged head bent and for the briefest, most terrible instant, Petra felt lips touch her palm.

The Thing screamed then, staggering back—"*Salt*! Salt—wicked girls, wicked!" Linette had staggered back too, in shock; Petra looked around desperately for her sister and found her standing a few feet away, her hands now balled into fists pressed against her tearstained cheeks—*tears!* Linette must have wiped them with her hand before they'd cupped their fingers together. Without conscious thought Petra sprang forward, snatched up the lantern, grabbed Linette by the elbow, and dragged her out of the clearing. The Thing screamed again, behind them; both girls ran frantically, paying no heed to the whipping branches that slashed at faces and arms, leaping with terror-fueled agility over thick undergrowth.

The sounds of panicked flight faded, leaving the clearing silent once more but for the gentle singing of water over stone. It appeared empty except for the fountain, but the shadows were deep in the dim starlight filtering down through the trees. A faint breeze scattered the tiny droplets that sparkled like diamonds on the carven viper eyes and sharp stone thorns.

Roses and Vipers was first published in the anthology Mother Ghost's Grimm Volume 2 in October, 2020.

LISA SHORT is a Texas-born, Kansas-bred writer of speculative fiction. She is a member of SFWA and HWA.

Weathering, the Storms of Time
Jenna Hanchey

When I finally stole the collar that opened portals in time, something unraveled within me. A piece of my spirit detached from my body, unwinding like a mist into the bitter cold. I felt lighter, as if I had finally dislodged the knot of frustrated desire that had long burdened my soul.

I straightened, gazing at my fearless expression in the King's own mirror, and carefully clasped the thick gold ring around my neck. The low light from the shaded lamp caressed my latest accessory, running lightly along its smooth curve before leaping from its surface to illuminate my violet waistcoat and mahogany breeches. I uncovered the lamp. There was no more need to hide; the end was at once the means, as the collar provided its own escape plan.

The clasp shut resignedly, pushing out air like a sigh.

Much as father derided my intellectual pursuits, I was no tactical fledgling. I knew exactly when and where to go first. Closing my eyes, I released the power nestled against my throat and felt the portal envelop me.

When my eyes opened, I was standing in my own chambers, a slight smile reflected in the mirror before me. No time to waste. I hurried to the desk, grabbing ink, paper, and seal, and scrawled a note. Before the wax could set, I was already leaping back through time once more.

As the golden portal expanded, I could just make out the door opening, my own past feet pounding into the room, before all was washed out by light.

I had been so angry that night. Bested at couplets—by a potential bride, no less—my father had laughed. And then, in front of the whole feast, King Salas the Third had shaken his head and bemoaned, "We have much work to do before you are fit to wear the crown."

Clenching my fists until nails cut into my palms, I spun around and stormed out, fleeing the wave of laughter breaking behind me. Halfway to my chambers, I began to cool. To reconsider. Perhaps it was just a joke. One that it would better to have taken in stride, one that was meant as playful rather than pointed.

Until I opened my door to find the note set upon my pillow, written in my own hand, fastened with my own seal. The note that reminded me what had been withheld from me, and instructed me how to claim it. I would show father I had what it took to rule. That I could rein in my feelings and do what needed to be done.

My second journey through the portal took no longer than the first, but I felt thinner, as if my being were stretched taut between the openings on either end of the portal. Panicking, I feared I would tear in two. But just when I spied a gilded seam beginning to slice through me, I snapped back together again..

I was still in my bedchamber, but it was different. Crisper. Not as many tapestries lined the walls; far fewer jewels graced the shelves. Now the real work began. I left a new note. One that I—or, the man I had been all those years ago—never received. But this time I would.

Again, I felt lighter. I stepped forward, testing my heft, and left a body-shaped cloud of glinting particles in my wake. I gasped and my heart seized, pulling me into a hunched position. When I could stand tall once again, the chamber was empty. No trace remained of the golden specks of light.

I hesitated before returning. My body felt unwieldy, and my blood seemed to slow to a stop, poised, as if to switch the direction of its flow within my veins. Should I really instruct myself to wed Vasta? She was beautiful, fit for a queen. Fit to make a man a king. But it was a sharp beauty, accentuated by pettiness and greed. A chord struck in my stilled heart as I remembered holding Mora's gentle arm before her death. Would that I had lost her to an accident! Then fixing the past would be simple. But no portal through time, no matter when I placed it, could save her from the kingdom-sweeping plague.

It could, however, cure mourning. It could draw me from my bedchamber, make it so that I did not waste years spilling impotent tears and penning sonnets for a love lost and life unlived. It could get me moving, married, and well on my way to being fit to be King.

Fit. I knew what my father meant. The words carried the weight of his judgment, even in jest, for the time I had whiled away on poetry and song, weeping and feeling. Holding tightly to my books when he called me to the map room, to the war room, to the council chambers. When he pushed woman after woman in front of me, flames to cauterize the wound.

I nodded decisively and entered the gleaming gap in time, blood suddenly coursing once more. Though in which direction, I did not notice.

What I did notice was that part of me did not arrive back in the present.

I felt the loss keenly, like my heart had been ripped from my chest. And perhaps it had. I looked down to find myself transparent. I could see the swirls of the handwoven rug through my legs. Or, no, it was not swirls on the rug, but within me. Pieces untethered, drifting apart.

My grief was gone.

And so was everything I had learned. Everything I had become in the learning. I reached for the memorized verses that helped soothe my lovelorn heart, to find a memory of their presence slowly fading. For the myths studied in a frenzy, attempts to locate the Underworld's gates that I might bring Mora back. Nothing. My panic lessened, evaporating along with my sense of for what I was searching. Even the memory I clung to—the night I sat vigil with father weeks later, after another wave of deaths. The night he clasped me in his arms and told me he was sorry to have lost her, too, that she would have made the best of queens. The one night his gaze fell warmly on me, a comforting blanket, as he told me he was proud of the man I had become, and he was certain I would weather this storm in time.

The memory began to drift out of reach. I unwittingly stretched out, trembling. I felt wrong as it became hazy, too light to remain on the earth. If only I could grab the past, claim it, turn it over in my hand! Let it settle again as a grounding weight upon my heart.

Instead, the moment winked out of existence, like it never existed.

Because now, it hadn't.

And without those years, without the anguish and grief and sorrow, neither had the person I'd become.

"You were wrong, Father," I whispered. "The storm weathered me, instead."

As my very being eroded, the golden collar slipped from my evanescing throat, fell through my fingers, and clattered loudly upon the floor.

JENNA HANCHEY is a critical/cultural communication professor by day and a speculative fiction writer by...uhhh...earlier in the day. Follow her adventures on Twitter (@jennahanchey) or at www.jennahanchey.com.

To the Water Goes My Pain
Addison Smith

From Draghtai's keep Raya escaped on stolen horse, stealing her life for herself and braving the world beyond. The beast galloped as if it too knew the pain of blade and glowing iron, the bruising of flesh and the breaking of bone. Raya gritted her teeth and clutched her broken hand, bleeding where she pried it from her shackles. She grinned, and her smile too was broken.

The forest loomed ahead and her mount hesitated. She urged it onward, into the growing thick where she could lose herself, find herself, remake herself. Even in her determination she feared the forest, the place her keepers said could only mean death. It was a threat they placed around her, further assurance she would never escape their great lord, he would held dominion over blood and pain and biting insect.

They approached the tree line and the horse fought her control. She cursed and yelled, and as they met the trees the horse reared high in the air. She spilled heavy to the ground, falling hard on knotted roots. Raya scrambled to avoid the horse's hooves and its sharpened shoes, but the beast cantered and kicked and left her. She watched after as it galloped back to the keep and away from the trees it so feared.

Raya ran crouched and cradling her broken hand, into the trees and away from Draghtai's vile sight. She ran until exhaustion took her and tears stung her eyes. Her feet tangled in vine and root and she tumbled down a long hill of rotting leaves. Her body struck rock and tree and she bit back her screams and the taste of blood. She fell all the way to the bottom of the hill where a shallow pool softened her final descent. She choked and splashed as the water filled her mouth, foul and strange. When finally she breached the surface, she lay in the pool and cried.

Draghtai would find her. She would be returned and branded and punished. She risked everything from her momentary respire and here she lay broken in a dark pool. She dared not move, because it would only confirm what she already knew. She would not walk from the pool. Her bones lay broken. Her breaths came shallow, coddling tender ribs, and she wept careful tears.

The pool warmed around her as if it could sense her pain. Come below, it offered, to a world where there is no more hurt. But Draghtai would not allow it. He controlled life, death, blood, and beetle. But the pool was warm and she let herself pretend.

The pool shimmered around her in cold moonlight and soon the darkness took her.

RAYA WOKE TO THE CARESS of the pool as it lapped over her skin. The forest lay still in darkness and hounds surely sought their missing captive. She rubbed at her eyes with soaking hands, removing the filth of the fall and of sleep and of tears. She rubbed until the water tickled on her lids and cleaned the mucus from her eyes. She held out her hand and stared. The blood was gone, washed away by the water, but so too was the pain. It was still broken. Even Draghtai could not mend bone so quickly. His healing was that of pain, bones bolted together to function in agony. Instead she felt the opposite. She squeezed at her wrist seeking out the fractures in her bone. She found them, but did not wince of cry. The pain was gone.

The water tingled on her eyes, a gift from the gods seeking to aid in her escape—holy water to deaden her pain. She stood from the pool with dark water at her knees lapping gently at newly-cleaned flesh.

She stepped from the pool, bare feet on leaf and earth, and made her way into the forest.

With freedom in her sight, Raya daydreamed as she trod through the wood. She stepped on clumsy feet, her gait plodding and spine bent. Beyond the forest, Lor'larum stood. The city bordered Draghtai's lands and kept him from escaping into the world at large. She would go to them for help. The pool gave her the strength, and though she hated to leave it had served its purpose. The water left a residue upon her skin and she brushed it from her body like thin leaves to the ground, flaking and falling. She shuffled onward toward Lor'larum, a smile not-so-broken on her face.

THE PAIN RETURNED. Hours passed and Raya stood among the trees wishing for the speed and ease of her stolen horse. The pain settled in her bones and Raya grew weary of fighting it. She brushed at her skin and still the flaking water fell from her, never fully cleaned from her body. Moonlight shone through the canopy above and pain racked through her body until she hobbled. It was not only the pain of broken bone and bruised rib, but a new pain. Her skin itself burned like a thousand arrows pocked her flesh.

The dream of Lor'larum did not vanish, but she succumbed to a baser need. She dreamed of the tiny pod and its numbing waters. She ached from relief from the pain that burned her body, punishment for leaving her master. Draghtai's reach was far and she knew the feel of his will. She had sat huddled among the biting beetles of his keep, seeking their pain over that which he would serve, knowing too that they were a part of him and his domain.

Raya crested a hill amid the forest, its top bathed in moonlight and inviting as the grace of gods. She stood within its light, praying the gods would aid her once more. She looked upon herself in the light. Her skin lay covered in white flakes, but they were not the strange water. Her skin died like paper and peeled from her body. She rubbed at her arms until they lay bare, and red and mottled skin shone through. It was another curse, and one she deserved for her desertion. She prayed the gods looked beyond her body, mangled and ruined, and aid her in her time of need. She pleaded that they heal her or numb her pain or bring her to Lor'larum where she could be free.

In the moonlight she spotted a glint in the trees. She smiled as she spotted it in the dark, the shimmering pool so like the one which took her pains. She praised the gods and stepped from the moonlight.

RAYA FELL. IN THE DISTANCE between moonlight and healing water she fell upon broken ankles and collapsed to the forest floor. She cried as pain stabbed through her body like chains and shackles and burning iron. She dragged herself through the thicket, desperate for the healing pond and the blessings of gods.

As she dragged upon her belly, her ribs sharpened around her lungs Her breath came in tiny gasps and her eyes filled with tears. She could not make it ten more feet, no matter how she tried. The pool was near.

Raya raked at the ground, broke nail and finger as she pulled her weight ever closer, knowing that all pains would be healed if only she could reach its waters. Draghtai made her resistant to pain. He bred her for this challenge, and so she would be lost to him.

She reached out her arm and screamed in pain. Her fingers rested on the edge of the pool, her fingertips wet and tingling in its holy water. She cried and they were tears of relief. With just that touch she knew she would live. She pulled herself forward until she fell and splashed into the water.

Raya floated upward, lying on her back as the pool tingled around her like tiny prickling legs caressing her body. She looked upon her breast and watched the water wash over her skin. It crawled and skittered, tiny beetles on tiny legs, biting and stinging and numbing her pain.

This puddle was older, more mature than the larva of the last. Raya laid her head back in the pool and smiled. It felt like home.

ADDISON SMITH writes weird science fiction, fantasy, and horror. His stories have appeared in *Fantasy Magazine, Fireside Magazine,* and others.

New Year's Skeleton
Larry Hodges

"*I*t *comes at midnight every year, every year, every year,*
It comes at midnight every year to find one to bestow."

Matt tried to ignore the New Year's carolers outside. Such superstitious nonsense! Besides, he preferred the original *Mary Had a Little Lamb* lyrics. Why mess with a classic? *Idiots*!

"Don't stay up late," his mom called from the staircase in the irritating, nasal voice that gave Matt indigestion, no doubt dressed in her perpetual night frock from two centuries past, with all the colors of charcoal. "It's almost midnight already. And for the love of God, beware the New Year's Skeleton!"

Matt laughed as he sipped a beer in the living room easy chair; he was on college break for a few more days. He'd already changed into his Spider-man pajamas, wrapped himself in a Superman bathrobe, and wore his Hulk slippers.

"The New Year's Skeleton is a myth the government made up so people wouldn't stay up late on New Year's Eve and get drunk," he said. "Well, I'm going to stay up late and get drunk." And read a book. Something scary. If only those idiots weren't so loud outside! And soon the fireworks would start . . . great.

"That's not what Aunt Maggie says," said the irritating, nasal voice. "She saw him once. Was lucky she didn't get picked as the heir."

"Aunt Maggie also says she saw Elvis. And ghosts."

"That was Elvis's ghost she saw, and if she says she saw Elvis, she did."

"So she sees skeletons, ghosts, and Elvis. Does she also see a psychiatrist?"

The door upstairs slammed.

Matt smiled and listened to the carolers for a moment.

"It's the New Year's Skeleton, Skeleton, Skeleton,
It's the New Year's Skeleton, its bones as white as snow."

White? Unless someone bleached it, wouldn't a skeleton have bits of rotting flesh hanging off it? Whatever. It astonished him that his mom believed these crazy things. But it wasn't really her fault; she and Aunt Maggie were hopelessly stupid. What next, Easter Bunny zombies? Tooth Fairy vampires?

"It finds a victim once each year, once each year, once each year,
It finds a victim once each year, and bangs him with a bone."

Would those *morons* outside please shut up? Shaking his head, he chose a book from the bookstand—*The Tell-Tale Heart and Other Stories* by Edgar Allen Poe. It had been a while since he'd read the cover story. Still sipping his beer, he was soon absorbed in it, could even hear the beating of the heart from under the floorboards, "...a low, dull, quick sound—much such a sound as a watch makes when enveloped in cotton." Louder! Louder! Louder!

A floorboard creaked. Matt turned his head just in time to say "*What the Hell*?" before the white bone smashed down on his skull. The one-armed glistening skeleton stood over Matt as he moaned, its left humerus bone held in its right arm. Matt sat up, rubbing his head.

"*See, I was right!*" Matt exclaimed, pointing at the bits of rotting flesh hanging off its bones.

The skeleton tossed aside its boney club and drew the long, serrated knife it had stuck in its ribs for convenience. It smiled in its skull-like way as it quietly went to work, ignoring the tell-tale screaming of its heir. After a few shrieks, the only sound was the carolers outside.

"Then it tears his flesh apart, flesh apart, flesh apart,
Then it tears his flesh apart, then leaves for parts unknown.
From this torn flesh bones arise, bones arise, bones arise,
From this torn flesh bones arise, and stands up on its feet.
The brand new New Year's Skeleton, Skeleton, Skeleton,
The brand new New Year's Skeleton, for one year, then repeat."

LARRY HODGES is an active member of SFWA with over 130 short story sales (over 170 if you include resales), 44 of them "pro" sales, including ones to Analog, Escape Pod, Flame Tree (4), Dark Matter (3), Daily Science Fiction (3), and 19 to Galaxy's Edge. Larry also has four SF novels, including "When Parallel Lines Meet," which Larry co-wrote with Mike Resnick and Lezli Robyn, and "Campaign 2100: Game of Scorpions," from World Weaver Press. Larry is a member of Codexwriters, and a graduate of the six-week 2006 Odyssey Writers Workshop and the two-week 2008 Taos Toolbox Writers Workshop. In the world of non-fiction, Larry is a full-time writer with 17 books and over 2000 published articles in over 170 different publications. Visit Larry at www.larryhodges.com.

The Nature of the Beast
Ed Ahern

The beast always ate him. George would stumble through the nighttime woods, thorns ripping at his skin, and without looking back would dream-see it bounding toward him. It was unlike any animal George knew—four legged, with clawed fingers rather than paws, a short, sharp-toothed snout, and a gray-black pelt. Twice his size. And somehow handsome.

It harried George like a sheep dog would, forcing him one way, then another. When George broke off to one side it would pounce and bite into his neck, almost ripping off his head. George felt hot, dry breath every time he died, shrieking in pain. George would then have to watch as the beast devoured him, Flesh, clothes and bones, all went into its maw.

He'd wake up screaming, clutching at his throat, and bathed in dank sweat. And poor Heather, undergoing cancer treatment they couldn't afford, would try to console him. After three consecutive nights of the same nightmare, his days were spent shaking and barely able to think, George started writing notes as soon as he came to. After his fifth dream death, George realized that he was always herded in the same direction, deeper into the woods, and that he could run further before dying if he kept to the way the beast was steering him.

That next night, before his getting devoured, he allowed himself to be steered to a cave opening at the end of a gully. He crawled in just before the beast could bite his feet, and pivoted to face his next death. But the beast settled on its haunches. A voice came from behind him.

"You really are a slow learner."

George spun around. A bulbous little figure sat on the cave floor, self-illuminated in a dim, hard blue light. "What's happening to me?" George yelled.

"You're still dreaming. Try and climb on top of your fear while we talk."

George squinted his eyes. Its face was- foxy? Certainly not human. "Can you protect me from that thing?"

"That thing is made in the likeness you gave it. If you'd been more twisted it could have been a vicious neighbor. Either way, it shepherded you to me."

"But... but why?"

The figure shrugged, blue light flickering. It had a pungent aroma, and George couldn't recall smelling anything in a dream. "Please focus on me. I have a quest for you, George."

"Quest? I'm not a knight, I'm an accountant."

The fox being sighed. "What you really are has been buried and needs disinterring. Think back to your childhood fantasies about battles and honor. That's who you want to be, and why your life seems to be an endless wait at an abandoned bus stop.

George's breathing had slowed to soft pants. "Look, ah, what should I call you?"

"Eltherel will do."

"Mr. Eltherel, I'm no hero, never even served in the military. You need a better candidate."

Eltherel waved a paw-like hand as snorts from the beast reverberated into the cave. "Now that you've reached me, George, these nightmares will cease. But your stultifying daymare will continue. Wouldn't you rather dare for fulfillment and great reward?"

Even in dream miasma, George tried to negotiate. "What's the quest?"

"One of our kind has gone rogue, killing several of my kind and yours. It sadly must be put down. If you can accomplish that, you'll be provided with a very large pot of gold."

"I'm not a killer."

"You could be for the right cause, you just haven't had a chance to demonstrate it."

"What's your pot of gold worth?"

"About four hundred twenty thousand of your dollars."

George frowned. "But it'll kill me instead."

"Perhaps, but if you really die, your next of kin gets the gold."

George hesitated, the pot held more than enough gold to pay off Heather's medical debts. "You're manipulating me."

The round little figure quivered as it shrugged. "Let's just call it a negative incentive. If you succeed this time there could be other quests with even bigger rewards and honor. Haven't you always wanted to do more than balance numbers?"

"That's just wrong. What are you?"

The being smiled wryly. "Not every fairy sits on a toadstool or dances around a fire. Some of us have to take responsibility for things."

"Why don't you do it?"

"We can't, George, there's a covenant that prevents us from harming each other. Disposal of other beings is a human nature."

"What are my chances of success?"

"Reasonable, perhaps seventy percent. We'll provide training in your sleep, but you'll have to face the renegade while awake, so real death is a possibility.

George frowned. "How would my wife get the gold?"

"It could be cash, gem stones, bearer bonds, whatever she'd be comfortable getting."

George sighed. "Seven out of ten. Crummy odds." He glanced back outside. The beast looked almost placid. Childhood memories swirled—of running on the roof of his house, of always taking on a fight, but also of being harshly disciplined until he learned to closet his nature. Urges stirred within him, pushing to be rebirthed.

What was worse, he wondered, than watching his wife suffer in poverty? He pushed concerns about his sanity aside. "All right, I'll do it."

"Excellent. Just excellent. Secrecy of course is required, and telling anyone else would only make you seem insane. If you succeed, we could provide other quests which will further enhance your essence."

"How can this monster you want me to kill exist in my world, Eltherel? He'd be trapped and caged."

Eltherel smiled sadly. His teeth were crooked and mossy. "You've already noticed that some people seem to you to be unfeeling and one dimensional, as if they weren't human? They sometimes aren't. We do have feelings, just not human ones."

"I guess I understand." George paused. "Is the beast outside really my creation?"

"All yours. And you're beginning to recognize that its nature is a reflection of what you want to be. Welcome back."

The Nature of the Beast was originally published in Nightmares and Phantasms.

ED AHERN resumed writing after forty odd years in foreign intelligence and international sales. He's had almost four hundred stories and poems published so far, and six books. Ed works the other side of writing at Bewildering Stories, where he sits on the review board and manages a posse of nine review editors. He's also lead editor at The Scribes Micro Fiction magazine.

https://www.twitter.com/bottomstripper
https://www.facebook.com/EdAhern73/?ref=bookmarks
https://www.instagram.com/edwardahern1860/

Harriers

A. P. Howell

Adal and Kuno moved toward the enemy encampment. They had run north to overshoot it by a generous margin, then cut west. Now they moved south carefully, noses to the wind, padding softly through the forest. The moon hung in a clear sky, a heavy waxing gibbous whose light painted leaves silver and puddled on ferns and logs beneath breaks in the canopy.

Adal could feel the moon's pull in his veins already: the change to wolf shape had come easily. Though it was still voluntary, instinct urged him that *this* shape was more natural and right than a naked ape. Kuno must feel the same pull, but it was not something one spoke of, not unless one was still a pup and surrounded only by the home pack.

Adal was many years from a pup. And a group of werewolves—even one so closely knit as his company's—might make for a pack of sorts, but not a home pack.

The wind carried the scent of humans: two of them, both male. Mere perimeter guards or scouts, their rank and role were of no particular importance. They were present, and that was all that mattered.

Adal and Kuno's mission was simple: kill.

Adal and the other werewolves attached to the company sometimes fought alongside soldiers in the field, but often scouted. They had speed, endurance, and the ability to gather valuable intelligence by scent. They could also fade into the wilderness more easily than humans, their bodies built for survival even in the absence of tools.

But as the campaign had continued, as their company broke off from the main forces to operate independently, the missions began to shift from intelligence gathering to harrying the enemy. There was a larger strategy at work. The Captain meant to delay their enemy from some rendezvous with allied forces, keep them unsettled and suffering a steady flow of small losses.

Few things unsettled soldiers so much as beasts with the minds of men.

Practiced in the art of stalking, Adal and Kuno separated and approached their enemies from opposite flanks. The men were alert—they had to know their assignment, whatever it was, placed them at risk. The pair moved quietly, for men navigating a forest by moonlight. Adal could smell the oil used to clean their weapons, but they had taken care to wrap and pad metal to minimize the sound of their movements. Adal crouched, waiting until Kuno had time to creep into position, and then he leapt.

The sudden movement startled both men and drew their attention away from their second attacker. Kuno knocked one to the ground before the man had a chance to identify the threat, much less draw a blade. Adal snarled at the other, lunging toward the man's flanks even as he attempted to face his four-legged opponent head on.

He drew his sword quickly, but Adal jumped and clamped his jaws around the man's wrist before he could bring the weapon to bear. Adal's teeth scraped against mail under the glove, but he jerked the arm mercilessly. The man cried out, as inarticulate as the man struggling beneath Kuno's bulk, and dropped his sword.

Adal bit a leg—more mail and another scream—and then twisted the man down. He bit a hand flung up to protect the vulnerable face and throat. No mail there, only leather, and bones crunched beneath the pressure of his bite.

Blood filled his mouth. He did not eat human flesh—to commit such an abomination would rightly earn him an ignominious execution—but the scent and taste of blood fired violent passions, especially this close to the full moon. The man's screams only added to the thrill, and whether that thrill owed more to the instincts of a wild beast or a solider, Adal could not say.

He was not so caught up in the moment that he failed to observe the man's gorget. It shone in the moonlight, thick and solid. Adal bit higher, savaging the screaming man's face and severing the carotid artery. Blood matted his fur as the man managed some gurgling noises and final convulsions.

It did not take long to end a life.

He raised his head to see Kuno stagger back from the second corpse. The air was filled with the scent of his blood as well. Kuno sank to the ground and, before Adal had reached him, he began the change, whimpering softly. Changing was, typically, merely uncomfortable; but the rigors of the change were painful to abused flesh and bone. As a man, Kuno hunched over, a hand covering his ribs.

"Got me with a knife," Kuno said. His voice was pained, but his breathing seemed normal: rapid, after his exertions, but without the wheezing or bubbling that might indicate a damaged lung.

Adal changed out of politeness, crouching naked beside his comrade. Changing helped ease injuries—soldiers welcomed that exchange for the increased pain—but they did not disappear entirely. Kuno was smeared with blood and it was difficult to tell how much was his and how much was the dead man's, but it appeared that his flesh had been slashed, not stabbed.

A rapid series of changes would only exhaust Kuno, far from camp and to marginal benefit. When the full moon rose, Kuno would have no choice: he would change into the form of a wolf. He would have to make do with the half-healing of his change, and perhaps stitches in his wolf's flesh, until the moon began to wane. Adal squeezed his shoulder in sympathy.

Kuno grimaced and nodded, then began his change. Adal followed suit more eagerly. Together, they made their way back to the company's camp, moving slowly in deference to Kuno's injuries. There was no hurry. Their night's work was complete.

The cooling corpses were a small reduction to the enemy's forces, but their comrades would sleep uneasily.

A. P. HOWELL's work appears in *Martian*, *Wyld Flash*, and *Underland Arcana*. Her website is aphowell.com and she tweets @APHowell.

A Life to Spare
Fulvio Gatti

The smell of moist wood overwhelms my centuries-old-numbed senses, while the chill grows into spikes of cold. The black wine cellar wall, destination of my desperate search among endless rows of massive time-worn barrels, loses cohesion before my eyes.

The haze soon reveals a shady figure covered in rags, unsettling blackness where a face should be, and chains rattling at his hips.

I'd pray, if I knew how.

"You are early, Predator," the Caretaker says.

I shiver. It feels odd. I've met him more times than I can remember, still he terrifies me.

"I know," I reply. "But you came anyway."

"You've been a good agent of Balance, Predator," he says. "Are you here to bargain?"

I push away a mental image of Nadia. She bounces a red ball against the wall and laughs in joy. The Caretaker must never know about her.

"I am."

The chains rattle in the dark. The icy cold metal wraps around the bottom of my jeans. The fabric rips. A hook sinks into my calf. Pain is just an echo.

The Caretaker stands still as random face features, eyes and noses, eyebrows and chins, flash and disappear.

"Tell me, Predator," the Caretaker asks. "Why do you want to change now?"

"I need it to survive."

"Did they discover you?"

"It happens. Only, today pictures travel so fast that it's impossible for a bloodsucker to stay hidden." I try to focus on a pair of green eyes. "That's why I already need a new face."

I barely keep from mentioning Nadia.

"I see you have already chosen the Life to Spare," the Caretaker says.

I groan. He saw her. "What's the point of this conversation, if you can read into me?"

If my bluntness annoys him, he shows no sign of it.

"There are rules, Predator," he explains. "You are here of your own free will. The Predator must choose a Life to protect. Swear to do it. Prevent any harm from being done."

That is the easy part. I don't need to feed on humans anymore.

"I'm willing to swear it."

The chains rattle, shaking me.

"So why are you hiding the truth, Predator?"

I stiffen. "Search me."

I'm tossed into the abyss, stripped away of my flesh. Sharp claws start scavenging my soul. When I find an invisible stalagmite, I grab it. I hold it tight. Part of me is still in the cellar, corporeal again.

"What happened to your last Life to Spare?" the Caretaker asks. "Her life cycle shouldn't be concluded yet."

Of course he doesn't read the news.

"She died of cancer." It's still painful to say it.

The Caretaker keeps silent.

"Unusual," he says. "Her lifeline showed no stains, twenty-nine years ago."

I scoff. "You'd be amazed by how fast humans can invent ways to kill each other—and themselves."

I try to move my legs, but the chains rise to tie them together.

"I can see the path to an exception, here," the Caretaker says. Sharp claws scratch my morale. "Alas, you must be honest, Predator. The untimely death of your Life to Spare is not the only reason why you came here ahead of time."

I hold my breath.

My thoughts brighten.

"My sole purpose is to protect, Caretaker."

The chains loosen.

"Please, present your new Life to Spare for proper exam."

My mind floods with pleasant memories of Nadia returning from school, singing a song from her favorite TV show, cuddling a kitten. The last image is her at the hospital, before her mother's deathbed, her eyes full of tears.

I've made a mistake.

The chains pull me down. I bang my face against the rocky ground. A tooth snaps out.

"I see a blood tie!" the Caretaker thunders. "You must spare a life out of pure selflessness, Predator! Anything else is against the rules!"

"We had no intercourse—I-I couldn't," I object. "I just want to protect the daughter as I did with her mother!"

Hooks pierce my hands.

A titanic weight crushes me.

"So you don't love Nadia, Predator?"

I see her mother, as a teenager, and then Nadia growing up. The same, big, irresistible brown eyes. I loved both of them. After her mother's death, I have fought hard to adopt little Nadia. If I vanish now, she'll go to an orphanage, or worse.

"Please," I whisper. "Let me live."

All that reaches me is silence.

"S-she needs me," I insist. The chains press on my lungs. Soon I won't be able to speak. "Just give me a few more yea—"

The voice of the Caretaker thunders.

"You broke the rules, Predator," he says. "But I can offer you one last chance."

"Please!" I yell. "I'd do anything!"

And then, I know.

"Would you give up on your immortality, Predator? Just for her?"

So, this is how it feels like. Sacrifice. The most surprising fact is that I'm now willing to do it.

I sigh. "Go on."

The rocky ground opens and swallows me. Haze and darkness now are one. I can't see, or move, or feel. Then, a million needles begin to pierce every inch of my skin. They rip me open, shatter me, turn me to ashes.

I dissolve into the hopeless void.

I wake up at the smell of moist wood.

I'm still in the wine cellar, yet there is something different in how the floor feels below my palms. A complete geography of scratches and bumps I now have access to for the first time.

I try to give a name to the pain in the calf. There are no chains to be seen, nor standing figures, but the ground by my leg is wet.

I touch it.

I smell it.

I taste it.

It's blood.

I flinch.

I feel suddenly, awesomely warm.

The injury will heal.

My new face has a round nose and high cheekbones.

Nadia will never know it, but tonight she lost her supernatural protector.

By earning a human father.

FULVIO GATTI is a speculative fiction ESL writer, SFWA member, from the wine hills of Piemonte, Italy.

Greenwich, Noon
Liam Hogan

I know when it is noon.

Though I am blind and dumb and kept in a small cell in the rafters of the Royal Observatory, I *know* when it is noon.

I know because at precisely that time a retired ship's surgeon will carve the day's date into my flesh. Each letter, each numeral, is a series of slashes of the knife. He cuts swiftly, with precision. The wound is then sprinkled with the "powder of sympathy", a pungent, acrid substance which reacts violently with my tortured skin and burns, and burns, and burns.

The surgeon, I think, is glad that I cannot scream.

Halfway round the world, they hope that the deep cuts they make in me are felt by my twin sister. We are part of a sea trial, she and I, an attempt to claim the prize promised by the Longitude Act of 1714. Her role as the seafaring twin was decided for her because she, though as blind as I am, can cry out as I cannot, and so alert the distant sailors aboard the schooner *Regina*, that it is noon here in Greenwich. By comparing this with their own, local noon, they will then know their longitude.

So goes the theory.

The sea trial will be deemed a failure, a relief perhaps to any other twins born to our abject poverty and equally lacking in those attributes by which they might otherwise be deemed human. For we are referred to not as people, but as dogs. That is how we are seen: two worthless lives, two souls so damaged from birth that until this cruel experiment began, we weren't even given names.

Now, they call me Sirius, after the dog star.

They call my sister Venus, the brightest of the wandering stars. They imagine her wandering across the oceans, looking to the dog star to know her place upon this Earth.

You must wonder how it is that I know what I know; how it is that I can even tell my story, when I lack the senses you take so easily for granted.

You assume, as does the surgeon, that because I am dumb I am also *deaf*.

You assume that because I cannot see, that I cannot *write*.

I have learnt the shape of your words. With my fingers I have traced the rough edges of the scars they leave on my skin. These have been hard lessons, every word carries the pain of cutting it into my flesh; this is how I order my thoughts, by the long, sharp strokes of an L, by the twist that tugs at the skin for the curve of a C, by the swift back and forth of an S. Each letter I know by how it feels to have it inscribed upon me, the lesson reinforced by the searing agony of the caustic powder with which my wounds are liberally sprinkled.

I am ignored by the surgeon, and by the two who throw rancid food into my cell and who all too rarely sweep the soiled straw from it. They are carefree with their words, these fools, for what does it matter what is said in front of one who cannot repeat what they say?

I think back to when my sister and I shared a filthy, infested bed in the hell in which we were raised, a hell that I now long to return to. She would croon to me, her awkward voice a balm against the kickings and the abuse that was always there, always sudden and always unforeseen.

When we were brought for the first time to Greenwich, and, for the first time, separated, I could still hear her through the thin walls of our cells, and I was not as concerned as I should have been.

And when she cried out in pain, when some terrible injury was done to her, I shared that pain, and thrashed and jerked in mutual torment. To the evident satisfaction of the great and good men there present.

If only I had stayed still, our fate might have been different and she would not be lost to me now.

My cell is quiet, when there is only me in it. If I lie still I can hear the conversations happening next door, or below. There is a great space there; once a week a crowd throngs, a meeting of the Commissioners of the Discovery of the Longitude at Sea, and the voices of the speakers are raised above the din of the multitude. From them I have learnt of the Prize that condemned my sister and I.

They talk about it incessantly, one crazed scheme after another. Sometimes they mention the *Regina*, and I know that these men, for all their fine learning and long words, do not know what I know: that the *Regina* will never return home, that it moulders at the bottom of the ocean.

I know this, because I have felt it. When my body was only half as scarred as it is now, I awoke breathless and panicky, a feeling that only intensified as I struggled to suck down the dank night air, as my bloodied hands beat upon the floor, until suddenly a bucket of my own filth was thrown over my shuddering form, a gaoler laughing at my plight. As the cold, rank liquid dripped off my face, I knew with more certainty than I have ever known anything before; that whatever small space my sister was confined to aboard the *Regina* it was flooded, and my sister was drowning.

I felt her anguish in every part of me, across the miles of ocean and land, I felt the pressure and the burning flames in her lungs as the ship surely sank.

Afterwards, as I sat huddled in a corner while my gaoler spat and kicked, I was consumed by an emptiness that hollowed me out from within, and I knew that for the first time ever, I was truly alone.

I could not comprehend why the surgeon still came the next day, and the next. How could he not feel it too? How could he not know?

The *Regina* is overdue. Fourteen months it has been gone. There are few parts of me left that remain unmarked by the passage of time, by the surgeon's knife. But still he keeps coming. Every day the surgeon cuts the date into me, sending an unheeded message to the bottom of the sea that it is noon here in Greenwich.

Today is the last such day.

Though I am blind, I hear the key in the lock as the surgeon opens the door, his footsteps as he approaches across the wooden floorboards. I know how long it takes between the lifting of the rags that cover me and the first cut of the knife. I smell his stale sweat and feel his hot breath and steel myself. The surgeon rests the point of the knife where he will make his first cut and exhales to steady his aim. With my left hand that I have wriggled free of my bonds, I reach out and seize his wrist, and with my other I twist and slam the sharp blade into his exposed throat.

I wait until I can no longer hear the drumming of his heels on the straw-strewn floor before I withdraw the knife. It does not take long.

Though I am mute, I inscribe my story—this story—for all to read, whether by sight or by touch, onto the body of the surgeon. I swiftly slash each neat letter, feeling the splash of the still warm blood spill onto my fingers, hearing the drip to the wooden boards at my feet. I hope, I *pray*, that it will drip all the way through to the congregation gathered in the great space below, as they sit there discussing balloons and cannon ships and the moons of Jupiter, and let those learn'd men know, that it is Noon, here, in Greenwich.

Greenwich, Noon was originally published/performed for Liars' League, Oct 2014.

LIAM HOGAN is an award-winning short story writer, with stories in Best of British Science Fiction and in Best of British Fantasy (NewCon Press). He's been published by Analog, Daily Science Fiction, and Flame Tree Press, among others. He helps host Liars' League London, volunteers at the creative writing charity Ministry of Stories, and lives and avoids work in London. More details at http://happyendingnotguaranteed.blogspot.co.uk

Shackled for Eternity
Kai Delmas

The drip of blood marks the passage of time. His own and that of the champions slain above.

He waits in darkness for those brave enough and skilled enough to pass the challenges. He shifts his bulk, chains rattle and rub against his raw flesh.

He waits for the one who will end this dark existence. For the one strong enough to defeat him.

Torchlight flickers from the hall beyond his prison. The chains compel him to fight. To protect what lies behind him.

The battle is brief. His wait is not over.

The drip of blood his only company.

KAI DELMAS loves creating worlds and magic systems and is a slush reader for Apex Magazine. He is a winner of the monthly Apex Microfiction Contest and his fiction can be found in Martian and is forthcoming in Tree and Stone and several Shacklebound anthologies. Find him on Twitter @KaiDelmas.

Chrysopoeia
Dawn Vogel

The alchemist claims he's turned lead to gold, but it's only sleight of hand.

When he pours the solution over the lead, time slows. No one else notices.

The liquid in his vials hides pyrite chunks, polished to gleam. His hand darts into the smoke of the reaction and removes the lead, so all that's left is a lump of gleaming "gold."

And then the masses crowd him, shoving money into his waiting hands.

He sells them vials of useless colored liquid, like the one he sold my mum.

Today, I'm front and center when he begins his routine, one of dozens staring up at him. If he looked closer, he'd notice it's not admiration in my eyes, it's anger.

He sets the lead on the table, tilts the vial over it.

I grab the lead before the liquid hits it, the pyrite an instant later.

His eyes go wide, but he moves as slowly as everyone else, too slow to beg me not to reveal his secrets.

When the smoke clears, I hold up lead in one hand, pyrite in the other. "There is no alchemy here. Only trickery."

The crowd disperses, disappointed.

"Give me that," the alchemist hisses, grabbing at my arms.

I turn, place both minerals on the table. "Take them. Leave before the authorities take an interest in your 'alchemy.'"

He sees my anger now and nods.

He won't trick folks here, like my mum, into quack alchemy cures anymore.

DAWN VOGEL lives in Seattle with her awesome husband and their herd of cats. Find her on Twitter @historyneverwas.

With Fire and Axes
DJ Tyrer

The Humans came with fire and axes.

The forest had been home to Elves since times immemorial, long before the Ogre Wars and the deaths of the Frost Giant kings. Down untold ages, Elves had held the dark woods against the horrors of the elder worlds and the more-prosaic threats of the latter times.

But, the days of the Elves were drawing to an end, their lives and culture in twilight, their numbers in decline.

And, as the Elves grew ever weaker, so their enemies had made greater and greater inroads into their realm. Literal roads – laid with the logs of butchered trees, reaching deeper and deeper into the ancient forest, like the greedy fingers of a grasping hand.

Ever closer to the forest's sacred heart...

It was here, in groves of evergreen oaks with trunks as broad as a dozen men and branches reaching skyward, that the very soul of Elven society could be found – in the most-literal sense, for these trees were the great Trees of Life upon which no acorns grew, but strange and peculiar fruits – ones like swollen amniotic sacs filled with a swirl of light and darkness – hung in clusters, each one holding the soul of an Elf waiting to be reborn. Waiting in numbers greater than the supply of bodies to house them.

Here, in these sacred groves, was the Elven race preserved through all perils and restored, reinvigorated, renewed. Here was the hope of ages, the constant of eternity. Here was the race made eternal in spirit.

For as long as the Trees of Life stood.

For as long as the Trees of Life stood...

But, somewhere in the Outer Darkness, beyond the walls of spirit erected by the earliest demiurges and many-limbed sorcerers of primordial times, strange and formless gods lurked, ever hungry for the light of life and the essence of Human souls.

And, O! how much brighter burned the eternal souls of the Elves, mocking the gods from within the protective Walls of the World; only the rarest Elf was ever slain in such circumstances that their soul could not reach a Tree of Life, but was swallowed whole by one of the gods, instead.

The gods lusted at the bountiful harvest that was ever beyond their reach – and, made pledges to the Humans who worshipped them in the fleeting moments of their lives, before their pitiful souls were swallowed up into nothingness.

Destroy the Elves, those cursed beings who mock you with their long years of life and repeated incarnations.

Tear down their forests, destroy their sacred groves, and you shall have power and health and glory.

And, the lords of Men listened to the whispers in their dreams, the dark promises, and redoubled their attacks, advancing with fire and axes, turning the forests to ash, and sending more and more Elven souls to hang like ripe fruit from branches in a patient wait for the creation of fresh bodies by the elders of their race.

Bodies too late in their creation...

"The Humans are coming!" went the cry. "The Humans are coming! Rally! Rally! Rally to defend the grove!"

It was a cry that echoed, again and again, between ancient trees that had known a world litten by a green sun and clouds shaped from marble and not from mist. Trees so old that even the bull-headed idols of ancient Udruk, forgotten even by the Jinn that haunted the sands that buried them, were but late-come in comparison. Trees that never had known a tumult in their vicinity since the very beginning of the world, not even when noisome Gbalbim had set out in its quest to corrupt all living things.

The trees shuddered a little at the clamour and activity, as if in fear, unless it were the fruit on their branches that quivered and shook, the souls within agitated at this peculiar disruption of their tranquil repose.

Battle raged nearby and blood was spilt. Sword clashed against sword and axe bit deep into shield. Spears tore open flesh and arrows flew with lethal accuracy. Men and Elves fell in desperate combat, the souls of the former escaping into the Outer Darkness, like dew evaporating beneath the merciless sun, to sate the hunger of their vile masters for just a moment, whilst those of the latter fled to the nearby grove to fill fresh fruits, each as helpless as an unborn child.

But, though their lives were ephemeral in comparison to those of the Elves, the numbers of Men were greater and the armies of Humanity overcame the defenders by sheer weight and, all too soon, the sacred grove was laid bare to their cruel work.

Destroy the Elves. Destroy their sacred groves.

The words whispered from beyond the Walls of the World spurred them on and the axemen and the spearmen set about their dreadful tasks. The fruit-like sacs that adorned the trees like festival lanterns were pierced by spearheads of iron, tearing open their diaphanous membranes and sending the souls contained within tumbling out of the world and into the waiting maws of the gods without. Trees tumbled, hewn apart by axe and wedge, and fire was applied, the garish dancing flames replacing the mystical glow of the trees.

Soon, the sacred grove was no more. Not an Elven soul remained.

"Come, men," called a leader emboldened, "more trees await the bite of axe blades. We'll show those Elves..."

And, so the war raged on.

And, beyond the Walls of the World, the gods feasted upon the intoxicating souls, like amber wine, and waxed in power... and the Walls cracked, just a little...

And, a little more...

And, the gods crouched ready in the darkness, waiting, for the moment when the Walls would fall and they would rush in like a black tide and devour not only the last of the Trees of Life, but every living thing in the world: Man, Elf, Ogre, plant, beast.

Come, glorious day – let us hunger no more.

DJ TYRER runs *Atlantean Publishing*, and has appeared in issues of *Sirens Call*, *Tigershark*, and on *Trembling With Fear*.

https://djtyrer.blogspot.co.uk/

Conscripted
Thomas J. Griffin

Henrik, son of Henrik lay upon his back, staring up at the moon. It would be the last he ever saw—his guts leaked into the grass from a gash in his belly—but at least it was full and bright.

He would not die alone. All around him lay friends and foes, a battlefield full of corpses. The man who'd cut him open lay not ten paces away, face down in the muck, the back of his head bashed in. They would be reunited soon in death, but for Henrik's part there would be no hard feelings. Such was the warrior's lot, to give one's life for lord and land, and he had given his full measure. They'd thrown back the invaders and won the day. He only wished his killer had given him as quick a death as he'd received. This dying was a hard business. The body clung to life until the last, the heart racing even as each pump spilled more blood upon the ground.

Across the field, a crow cawed and took flight. Henrik's foggy eyes followed it through the dark, then marked more movement upon the ground. Someone was making their way through the carnage toward him. Robed and hooded, they moved with care but not fear, stepping over and around the dead, occasionally stopping to crouch over a body, possibly checking for signs of life.

When they were close enough, Henrik called out. His voice was weak, his mouth dry, but he managed to get their attention.

"Hail, brave warrior," the robed figure said. A woman's voice, with a music to it that pricked the ear. Drawing close, she knelt beside Henrik, and by the light of the full moon he could see her face. She was young in feature, but missing youth's vigor, her skin washed pale, her eyes bruised from sleeplessness. Thin wisps of ashen hair framed her face beneath the hood. She smiled at Henrik, but it was not a happy look.

"Water?" Henrik asked, his eyes on the full skin hanging by a loop from her shoulder. His tongue felt like cotton.

The robed woman nodded. With one hand she brought it to his lips while the other cradled the back of his head, pressing gently forward so he could drink. The water was cool and he drank greedily, though it had a strange, sweet aftertaste he did not care for. When he'd had his fill, she rested him back upon the grass. Her gaze traveled the length of his body, noting the wound in his middle, then met his eyes intently.

"Shall I help to ease your passing, brave one?"

Henrik swallowed, savoring the last of the moisture, then nodded. "I'm ready," he said, tears forming. "I've met a warrior's end... I will go proudly to the hall of my fathers."

The robed woman dropped her smile. "Not just yet."

She was quick with the knife, the blade plunging into Henrik's heart before he had time to fear it. The shock lasted but a moment, as did the pain. Then his eyes faded, his last sight of the robed woman, and the full moon hanging over them both.

"AWAKEN."

Henrik, son of Henrik was surprised to find his eyes open. How long they'd been closed, he did not know, but the moon above him was now banked in cloud.

"Rise."

Across the battlefield, hundreds of fallen warriors stood up from death, and Henrik rose with them. They were a pale troop, drained of life's color, but then, it was no longer their lifeblood which animated them. Turning, Henrik spotted the robed woman atop a far hill overlooking the field, arms outstretched, fingers splayed. She glowed with a negative light, too bright to look at yet too dark to see, and when she spoke it was with an irresistible music. Henrik had no choice but to listen.

"Brave warriors, you have done well this day, but your task is not yet complete, your families not yet safe. The invaders still defile our land. Even now they regroup at their ships, planning their next raids."

No, thought Henrik desperately, *let me die*. This was no longer his fight. He was filled with a weariness to turn his bones to sand, his guts still hanging from him like scarlet rope. Yet, though his mind willed it, he could not lie back down. The most he could manage was to turn his head. All around him, an army of pained faces and hollow stares echoed his plight.

"We go now to meet our foes at the shore and drive them back to sea. They will not expect us. Let us finish this night what we have begun, for lord and land."

It was that voice. It held Henrik up, filled him with a purpose not his own, and so long as it did, he knew he could not rest. His eyes returned to the robed woman as she issued her final command.

"March."

THOMAS J. GRIFFIN edits for *Flash Point SF* and writes out of an attic that could use more natural light.

Don't miss out!

Visit the website below and you can sign up to receive emails whenever Eric Fomley publishes a new book. There's no charge and no obligation.

https://books2read.com/r/B-A-PMCT-JVXBC

BOOKS 2 READ

Connecting independent readers to independent writers.

Lightning Source UK Ltd.
Milton Keynes UK
UKHW040646051222
413345UK00005B/793